Giada De Laurentiis's
Recipe for Adventure
Hong Kong!

written with Taylor Morris
illustrated by Francesca Gambatesa

Grosset & Dunlap
An Imprint of Penguin Group (USA) LLC

To my sister, Eloisa, with whom I first explored the
beautiful city of Hong Kong . . . and who taught me that even
though the world is one giant adventure map begging to be
explored, the biggest treasures are always at home!

这本书是献给我的姐姐，埃洛伊萨，我与他第一次访问香
港美丽的城市。我从她的世界是一个大冒险乞讨被发现，
但在家里，你总能找到最伟大的宝藏！

GROSSET & DUNLAP

Published by the Penguin Group

Penguin Group (USA) LLC, 375 Hudson Street, New York, New York 10014, USA

USA | Canada | UK | Ireland | Australia | New Zealand | India | South Africa | China

penguin.com

A Penguin Random House Company

Chapter 1

"What kind of food do you think they eat in Peru?" Alfie asked his sister as they sat at the family computer in the living room and researched world maps, customs, and foods from around the globe. "I bet Zia Donatella's been. We could ask her to tell us stories from there!"

It'd been months since Alfie and his sister, Emilia, traveled to Paris and even longer since their trip to Naples. Although *traveled* may not be the best word for what happened.

They still didn't really understand it, but their adventures most definitely had something to do with their great-aunt Donatella, the food she cooked, and the stories she told them. Alfie and Emilia couldn't wait for their next adventure. Only this time, they hoped they might get to help choose their destination.

"No, let's go to Greece," Emilia said, pointing to the screen as she clicked the mouse. "Someplace like this island called Santorini. Look at those white buildings and perfect blue water!"

"Or maybe someplace crazy different, like Morocco," Alfie said, clicking away from the Greece page.

"Go back! I was looking at that."

"Hey, kids," Dad said as he came into the living room. "What are you doing? Planning our next vacation?" Little did he know that they were trying to plan a trip, only it didn't involve him or their mom. It was always just Alfie and Emilia who traveled, which was sometimes scary but always an adventure.

"Just looking at maps," Alfie replied. He really did love maps, so it wasn't strange for him to be studying one on-screen.

"Alfie, are you still going to help me clear out the garage this weekend?" Dad asked.

Alfie had forgotten he'd promised to help his dad. "Well, I was going to play soccer on Saturday," Alfie said.

"What about you, Emilia?"

"Sorry, Dad," she said. "I'm working on a school project that's due Monday."

"Sheesh, you two," Dad said. "Way to ditch the old man."

Alfie didn't notice when Dad left the living room because he and Emilia went back to fighting over control of the computer. Emilia's next idea was to travel to Belize; Alfie was now thinking about India.

"Kids! Who wants a snack?" they heard their Zia Donatella call from the kitchen.

Emilia could have the computer—Alfie was off to see what Zia was making.

"What kind of snack?" Alfie asked as he entered the kitchen with Emilia close behind.

"How about some pancakes?" Zia said. Her long salt-and-pepper hair was piled high on her head and held up with two red chopsticks.

"After dinner?" Alfie asked.

Emilia didn't seem to care since she was already at the refrigerator, ready to help. "You need the eggs, milk—Alfie, get the flour and sugar from the pantry."

They'd made all kinds of pancakes on Sunday mornings, and both Alfie and his sister could make them—from scratch—on their own.

"No, no, not that kind of pancake," Zia said. Even though it was the end of the day, Zia was still dressed beautifully in wide-leg tomato-red pants with a fitted blouse and a necklace of several long, shiny golden strands. Alfie knew that his sister loved Zia's easy style. "All we need is the flour. Plus a little warm water and a little cold."

"That's it?" Alfie asked. "What can you make with flour and water?"

"A thousand things! They are a magic combination on their own, but I do have one secret ingredient," Zia said. From the refrigerator, she pulled out a bunch of something long and green. "Scallions!" she said triumphantly. "They're like onions but have a much milder flavor. Now hand me that bowl," she said, pointing to the blue bowl on the counter.

"So, Zia," Alfie said as he passed the bowl to her, "where does this dish come from?" In other words, where were they going next?!

"Oh, lots of places." She mixed the flour with some cold water, then added warm water from the tap. Suddenly, what had been a pile of fine flour became firm, round dough. Magic, just like Zia had said.

"Yeah, but where did you learn this recipe?" Emilia asked eagerly.

"What recipe?" Mom came into the kitchen, followed by Dad.

"Cooking again, Donatella?" Dad said. "That big dinner wasn't enough?"

Earlier that night, the whole family pitched in to cook a dinner of chicken *piccata* with a side of asparagus, cherry tomatoes, and mozzarella. Alfie didn't even have to be asked to slice the fresh cheese, and Mom taught Emilia how to tell when the chicken was cooked through. Since Zia arrived, they had become quite the sous-chefs.

"Just a little treat from my days in China," Zia said.

Alfie and Emilia looked at each other. "China!"

"Who wants to slice the scallions?" Zia asked, and before Alfie could jump to it, Dad was already around the counter, knife in hand.

"I hardly ever get to help out," he said as he started on the scallions. Alfie slumped back in his seat.

"Zia, you're always telling the kids about your travels," Mom said. "Tell us all a new story."

"Like, what's the coolest thing you saw in China?"

Alfie asked, leaning on the counter.

"Do you think dragons are cool?" Zia asked, raising an eyebrow.

"Uh, yeah!" Alfie said. "But you didn't really see dragons, did you?"

"I most certainly did, dancing down the streets," Zia said. "Lions, too."

Alfie and Emilia looked to their parents for confirmation that Zia was pulling their legs. Dad shrugged as he finished with the scallions. "Presto!" he said, setting his knife down.

As she turned out the dough on the counter, Zia said, "Hong Kong was magical, and I loved being there since it's by the water like my home, Naples. The Chinese believe water brings harmony and prosperity into life." Zia rolled out the dough into a long, flat oval shape. Then she brushed it with sesame oil. "The food in Hong Kong even reminded me of Italy, at least *un poco*, a little."

"Really? How's that possible?" Alfie asked. He'd

ordered plenty of Chinese takeout, and none of it remotely resembled Italian food.

"You don't think Chinese noodles are a little like spaghetti?" Zia asked. "Or dumplings a little like ravioli?"

Alfie had never thought about that before, but now that Zia mentioned it, he saw her point.

"Now for the scallions," Zia said. She tossed a small handful onto the dough. "*Allora, aiuta.* Help." Alfie hoped this meant that they might soon be off to China, and he started feeling excited. But as soon as Dad grabbed the bowl of scallions, Alfie got a bit annoyed. He'd been traveling the world with just his sister—he definitely didn't need (or want) his parents tagging along now.

"Dad, I got it," Alfie said, putting his hand in front of his dad to stop him from adding more.

"Hey, can't I help this time?" Dad asked.

"Some red pepper flakes might be good, too," Zia said, sprinkling some over the top as Dad finished with the scallions. Zia then rolled the dough up so it looked like a snake, cut it into thirds, then rolled each of those sections around like a cinnamon bun. "Who wants to have a try smashing one into a pancake?"

"I do!" Alfie called, but before he could get to it, his dad pounded the side of his fist down into the dough.

"Perfect!" Zia said, flattening it out even more. They did the same to the rest of the dough sections, and Zia fried them, one by one, in a hot pan with vegetable oil. They came out golden brown and smelled of sweet onion.

As the family ate the snacks—slightly crispy on the outside with a mild onion flavor and a hint of red pepper—Alfie figured that, unfortunately, they weren't going anywhere. Would he ever get another chance to taste the special food Zia made from China?

Chapter 2

Alfie couldn't sleep. Every time he felt himself dozing off, another thought popped into his head, as if his brain didn't want him to relax. Since he couldn't keep his eyes closed he stared at the map of the world on his wall.

He decided to get out of bed. Maybe he'd get back on the computer and look up the big cities of China, like Beijing, Hong Kong, and Shanghai, or other places in the world he might want to see.

He headed into the living room, but before he could get on the computer he noticed a dim light coming from the kitchen.

"Hey," he said, finding Emilia leaning over the plate of

leftover scallion pancakes. "What're you doing?" He sat on a stool opposite her and helped himself to one of the other pancakes.

"Can't sleep," Emilia said, taking a bite.

"Me, either," Alfie agreed. He bit into the pancake—it was still crispy and filled with the slightly sweet flavor of the scallions. "I just keep staring at my map and thinking."

"About China?"

Alfie smiled through another bite. "Maybe. And dragons and lions. You think Zia was teasing us about all that?"

"No way," Emilia said. "She doesn't need to exaggerate her stories."

"True," Alfie said, thinking. "What about Mom and Dad helping out with the pancakes?"

"I know!" Emilia said. "Dad was, like, all over it!"

They sat quietly for a moment. Lowering his voice, Alfie said, "Do you think Zia was trying to, you know, send us on another adventure?" It was something they only talked about in whispers, and *only* to each other.

"I thought so," Emilia said. "But who knows? We've had tons of food from all over the world over the past few months from Zia, and we haven't gone anywhere since Paris. We still don't really know how this works."

"Or when it'll happen," Alfie said.

"But China would be cool," Emilia said. "Zia said the

food in Hong Kong kind of reminded her of Italy."

"It'd be fun to go someplace so different from home." Alfie pictured it all in his mind again. "I mean, I've seen pictures of China but to be there, in the mix with all those people . . ."

". . . hearing the language and seeing signs written with Chinese characters . . ."

". . . and tasting the food . . ."

Alfie and Emilia were lost in their thoughts of China. As they took their last bites of the scallion pancakes, they got that strange but familiar feeling in the pits of their stomachs, like being on a roller coaster that suddenly drops . . .

Chapter 3

It happened quickly. One moment they were sitting in their kitchen at home over a plate of scallion pancakes, and the next they were standing on a street in a foreign city, just like when they went to Naples and Paris. The light from neon signs hanging above and around them lit up Emilia's face as Alfie watched her take it all in. Strings of lights were draped festively across the street from one side to the other, red paper lanterns hung from awnings, and the sidewalk was packed with more people than Alfie had ever seen. And then he saw a dragon in a window across the street. It was long and skinny like a snake but as tall as his dad. Its scales were bright orange and green

and were made of some kind of thin material.

"I think we're in Hong Kong," Emilia said breathlessly. Alfie knew that already, looking at the dragon—just like Zia had said, but not at all like Alfie had imagined. "The signs," Emilia continued. "They're in Chinese characters and in English."

She was right—they were surrounded by signs in two languages. He hadn't noticed right away—the abundance of things to see and the people all around was overwhelming.

But Alfie wasn't overwhelmed—he felt incredibly excited. Excited and ready to start their adventure— getting their bearings, discovering places to eat, and finding a friendly face to help them get around. Just like they'd done in Naples and Paris.

"You're here!" a voice called from down the street. A girl emerged from the crowd. She wore a red tracksuit and had her black hair pulled back in a tight, low bun. She looked to be about Alfie's age, and she carried a gym bag over her shoulder that was almost as big as she was.

When she stood in front of them, she looked relieved. "I am so glad. Mother and Father would not be happy if I lost you."

"You ... know us?" Emilia asked.

"You are the foreign exchange students? From America?" the girl asked. "I was supposed to pick you up but lost track of time. Please don't tell my parents. They'll be so mad if they know I was at the gym late," she said. "C'mon, let's go inside."

The girl opened the door that Alfie and Emilia stood in front of, which they hadn't noticed. The sign above the door wasn't illuminated, but Alfie could still see the English writing. THE GOLDEN LION, it read.

Inside, warm air engulfed them. It turned out the Golden Lion was a restaurant—more than a dozen tables filled the space. The ceilings were low but the light glowed warm and bright, and the walls were painted a bright orange-red. The kitchen in the back was open, and Alfie could see the shiny steel appliances and counters from the doorway. There was a fish tank along the dining-room wall with several brightly colored fish of all sizes swimming lazily among the aquarium plants.

But between the kitchen and Alfie sat a mass of people all gathered around several tables in the center of the room—and everyone sitting there stared back at them.

"You made it!" a woman said, walking toward them with a smile spread across her round face. "Ying found you okay, then. Was the walk from the station all right?"

Alfie felt his head nodding yes. "Yes, it was fine," he said. He knew from their other adventures that it was best to go along with things.

"Good," the woman said. "Normally we can't pull Ying away from her gymnastics. I was almost afraid she would leave you wandering the streets of Hong Kong alone!"

The girl dropped her gym bag and walked toward the table—but not before pausing behind her mother's back and winking at Alfie and Emilia.

At the mention of Hong Kong, though, Alfie now knew

what city they had landed in! And Ying—that must be the girl's name.

"Everything looks delicious," Ying said, taking a seat at the table. "I'm so hungry."

"Yes, come in, come over," the woman said, guiding them to the table. "We are so happy to be hosting you, especially here in our restaurant. Come meet my husband."

"Hello," a man said, standing up and coming toward them.

Alfie thought he remembered that, in China, it was customary to bow to one another. As the older man got closer, Alfie bowed from the waist. Emilia picked up on what her brother was doing, and she did a little curtsy. While his head was still down, Alfie heard giggling coming from the table. The man had his hand outstretched for a handshake, and several people at the table—including Ying—were quietly laughing.

"Ying!" the mother snapped. Ying quickly stifled her laugh, and the others at the table quieted down, too. "Shaking hands is just fine," the woman said. The man had a smile on his face that crinkled the corners of his eyes. He nodded toward his hand, and Alfie shook it. He had a light grip.

"Welcome to our city and our restaurant," the man said. "We are so happy to have you. Here, have a seat." He offered Alfie a chair; Ying sat next to him and Emilia sat next to her.

"Thank you very much, Mister . . . ?" Alfie said.

"Oh!" The woman put her hand to her chest as she took her seat. "Our manners—I am sorry. We didn't even introduce ourselves. But no mister or missus, please. Since you're staying with us, as family, you can call me Aunt Chan. And you may call my husband Uncle Wu. Does that sound okay?"

"Yes, thank you," Alfie said. "I'm Alfie and this is my sister, Emilia." No one made a move to eat and he felt like everyone was staring at him, waiting for him to do or say something. "Is this your restaurant?" he asked, taking another look around. One wall was covered with a bigger-than-life painting of a lion—golden, like the restaurant's name. The face didn't look ferocious—more like a happy dog.

"Yes, it's ours. We are not quite open yet," Uncle Wu said. "But we are very excited."

"Just three days until the grand opening," Aunt Chan said.

"You're here at the perfect time," Ying said to them. "And not just because of the restaurant opening and the fact that schools are closed. It's New Year's Eve!"

"New Year's Eve? But that was a month ago," Alfie said, confused.

"No, it's today," Ying said. "Do you know about the Chinese calendar? It's based on the lunar and solar cycles."

"Yeah, we might have learned something about that in school . . . ," Alfie tried, but the truth was, he didn't know.

"Didn't the agency give you any information before you came?" Aunt Chan asked. "It's the *Chinese* New Year. The Spring Festival! The most important week of the year, and tonight is the beginning!"

"Did you think all this was for you?" Ying smiled, nodding to the table and people and food, but Alfie got the feeling she meant to be playful.

"I think we should eat," Uncle Wu said.

"Agreed!" Ying cheered.

Alfie agreed, too. And when he saw how much food was on the table, he couldn't wait to taste every single dish.

Chapter 4

"First, this is—well, the family," Aunt Chan said. One by one she introduced each guest. "This is my brother, Li; his wife, Ping; my sister, Shan and her husband, Luo; their two kids, Yan and Xiao Chen. These are Uncle Wu's brothers—they're twins—Wen and Ming . . ."

There was no way Alfie could possibly remember all the names. Ying must have seen it in his eyes because she said, "Don't worry. We won't quiz you."

"Let's eat!" Aunt Chan said. Alfie could almost hear Zia saying *mangiamo*, which meant the same thing.

Everyone began passing dishes and piling food on their plates. Alfie let his eyes roam slowly across

the table—the dishes of food, many of which he didn't

recognize, created a rainbow of color. Alfie considered

himself pretty skilled in the art of ordering Chinese

takeout, but he'd never seen a spread like this. There was

a huge bowl full of rice, whole tangerines so rich in color

they were almost red, eggrolls, a whole fish (head, tail,

eyes, and all!), a platter with eight little compartments

full of colorful foods—in whites, reds, oranges, and

more—another plate piled high with leafy greens and long beans, plus dumplings, which Alfie had to admit did look like raviolis, as Zia Donatella had said. The sight of it all made his stomach rumble.

Luckily, the family didn't expect Alfie and Emilia to know about every Chinese dish, so they pointed out the things they might not know, like the red melon seeds and the kumquats, which looked like miniature oranges. Emilia thought she was filing up on dumplings, but Ying told her it was actually something called *gok jai*.

"They look like dumplings," Ying explained. "But they're richer. They have different fillings like peanuts, coconut, and sesame seeds, and they're deep-fried."

"Everything is better deep-fried," Emilia said. Alfie was glad to see that sitting next to Ying and preparing to dive into a plateful of exotic food was helping her relax. She'd been pretty quiet so far.

Alfie was ready to eat, too. Once his plate was full, he reached for his fork. But instead of a fork there was a pair of chopsticks. And Alfie had never really mastered them. They always came with their takeout or were offered on the tables of Chinese restaurants, and he had tried to use them once or twice. But it was hard and he always got frustrated, so he normally just dug in with a fork. Now, that wasn't an option.

He picked up the red lacquered chopsticks that sat near his plate. He tried to hold them between his fingers like the others did, but they immediately tumbled onto the table. He tried holding one chopstick in each hand to grab a dumpling—he almost had it to his mouth, but it slipped away at the last moment. Feeling like everyone was watching and wanting to prove that he could eat with them, Alfie took both chopsticks in his fist and speared a dumpling. That's when the entire table let out a gasp.

"No, never, never stab your food," Aunt Chan said.

"I'm sorry," Alfie said, feeling panicked at the response.

"It's okay, Alfie," Uncle Wu said. "We'll teach you how to use your chopsticks. It's just, in our country, we see spearing your food as, well—disrespectful."

"And bad luck," Aunt Chan said. "And with the restaurant opening, we want to make sure that only good luck visits us. We have many customs here that you may not know about, especially during the Spring Festival, but we will help you understand exactly why they are important to us."

"I'll show you how to use the chopsticks," Ying said. "It's easy!"

"I bet you've been using them since you were a baby," Emilia said.

"Just about," Ying said. "Start like this: Rest one chopstick in the crook between your thumb and first finger and let this part rest on your ring finger. Then, hold the other one with your middle and first finger and use your thumb to help keep it stable. The trick is, the bottom chopstick never moves. See?" She wiggled her chopsticks like an alligator's mouth and Alfie realized she was right—the bottom one didn't move.

From there they learned the art of slurping long noodles. It was another superstition to never cut or break long noodles, which represented prosperity. Alfie and Emilia had fun making noises slurping them up as the broth splashed in their faces. Mom would have had a fit!

The table settled into eating. Alfie struggled with his chopsticks, but he managed to find ways to get the food into his mouth—without being disrespectful.

"It's so cool you're opening a restaurant," he said as he bit into a piece of chicken.

"Thank you," Aunt Chan said. "We're nervous but excited." She sounded more nervous than excited.

Uncle Wu must have sensed it, too, and quickly added, "It's going to be great. We moved from the countryside years ago to open a food stall on Temple Street," he explained to Alfie and Emilia. "We had it for years, and it was very popular..."

"The most popular," Ying said.

Uncle Wu smiled. "Well, one of the most popular, so we decided to make the leap from a street food stall to a restaurant. It's been a dream of ours for some time."

"Mother is worried about the dreaded Mrs. Liu," Ying said with a strange look in her eyes, like she was speaking of a monster.

"Who is Mrs. Liu?" Emilia asked. A piece of fish dropped from her chopsticks, and she patiently started picking it up again.

"She's this famous—or should I say infamous—Hong Kong restaurant reviewer," Ying explained. "But she doesn't come in and eat the food then write about it like most reviewers. She makes all these crazy requests."

"Like having something cooked at an exact temperature," one of Uncle Wu's brothers said.

"I heard she gave a restaurant a bad review because

she didn't like the decorations," Aunt Chan's sister-in-law said. "She didn't even taste the food."

"It's true," Ying said. "She'll ask for this sauce with that meat, or this on the side and that on a different plate, or no foods touching each other."

"Those are just rumors," Uncle Wu said. "She challenges every restaurant to have the best food and service possible."

"She sounds a little crazy," Alfie said.

"Not crazy," Uncle Wu said. "But demanding, yes."

"And very influential," Aunt Chan said. "She writes for the *Hong Kong Dining Authority,* which is very respected and used by both tourists and locals. She can make or break a restaurant."

"As you can see," Ying said, "everything has to go *perfectly.*" She said it as if she'd heard the phrase a thousand times.

Aunt Chan continued, "We have no idea when Mrs. Liu will come in, so we have to be ready at all times."

"And we'll teach you all about Chinese cooking while you're here, too—if you want to learn," Uncle Wu said.

"I do!" Emilia said.

Alfie wanted to learn, too, but mostly by eating.

The feast was topped with a cake made with sticky rice and sweetened with brown sugar. Alfie had seconds, he liked it so much. His belly was full, the family was so nice, and Emilia had settled in with Ying.

"Thanks for everything," Alfie said. "Our first night was amazing." He wondered how far their home was, what his room would look like, and how soon he could go to bed. Being so stuffed made him sleepy.

"*Was* amazing?" Aunt Chan asked. "Ying, are you ready for bed?"

"Bed?" Ying said. "The night is just getting started!"

"There's more?" Emilia asked.

"Lots more," said Ying.

Chapter 5

Everyone headed to the door and put on their coats.
Alfie and Emilia slipped into items lent by Ying's family.
Ying's parents had been a bit confused by the fact that
Alfie and Emilia had arrived without suitcases, but
there was so much activity trying to get everyone out
the door that they seemed to have forgotten. Ying told
them they were going to the big New Year's Eve parade,
and as they walked through the brightly lit streets, Emilia
said quietly to Alfie, "This is the way to do it—being fed,
staying with a family who was somehow expecting us.
We don't have to worry about anything. And I like Ying,
don't you?"

"Yeah, she's cool," Alfie said. "Maybe Zia is finally perfecting her magic."

The group walked down the busy city streets jam-packed with people out for the celebration, cars slowly passing by, the sidewalks lit by the signs of the many businesses and restaurants they passed. Alfie couldn't help bumping shoulders with people as they walked the busy street, and he kept offering apologies to each person.

Ying laughed. "Don't bother. They don't even notice you; it's too crowded."

But Alfie did notice everybody enjoying the festive air—large groups of friends and families walked together in packs, talking loudly, laughing, and looking happy.

"We're headed to the ferry to go across to Kowloon and Victoria Harbor," Ying said. "Have you ever looked at a map of Hong Kong?"

"I haven't, but I'm sure Alfie has," Emilia said. "He loves maps."

They turned onto a street that was totally open to pedestrians, so they walked down the center with no worries of cars.

"Right now we're on Hong Kong Island," Ying explained. "That's where we live and where our restaurant is. But there are four parts to Hong Kong: Hong Kong Island, Kowloon Peninsula—where we're going now—New Territories, and then Outlying Territories, which are all the other little islands around the harbor and sea area. We're going to take the world-famous Star Ferry to get to Kowloon. There are other ways to cross the harbor, but going by ferry is the most scenic."

The ferry pier was jammed with people all making their way through the turnstiles and onto the waiting boats.

"Everybody stay together!" Aunt Chan called out.

Emilia lost her grin and she looked around with wide eyes. Alfie hooked his arm through hers. "I'm here," he said.

Moments later they stepped across the wide metal plank and aboard the green-and-white boat. Ying led the way up onto a deck with rows of connected wood-and-metal chairs facing forward like a movie theater. Windows ran along the entire length of the boat, giving everyone a view of inky black water and the sparkling buildings beyond.

"Do you want to sit inside or go stand by the railing?" Aunt Chan asked the kids.

They looked at each other and in unison said, "Outside!"

As the boat slowly pulled away from the pier, Alfie and Emilia were treated to an incredible view of the harbor and the area of the city called Kowloon. Skyscrapers lined the edge of the water, their lights twinkling like stars in the evening sky. Other boats dotted the harbor; several green-and-white Star Ferries headed back the way they'd just come, wooden boats with sharp prows and red masts, and small motorboats all jockeyed for space in the crowded waters.

Suddenly, they heard music coming from somewhere.

"How lucky!" Ying said. "We're in time for the Symphony of Lights! Look!" She pointed across the harbor at the buildings. As the music played—from speakers along a promenade in front of them and the pier behind them—beams of lights rose from the tops of several of the skyscrapers. Diamond-shaped patterns

ran up the full length of one building, a hot pink stripe wiggled up and down another. Blue lasers shot out from the other buildings, dancing in the black sky, and it was all in rhythm to the music.

"Is this for New Year's Eve?" Emilia asked, her eyes wide as she watched the lights fill the sky.

"Actually, it happens every night," Ying said. "It's great, isn't it?"

"It's so cool," Alfie said. Hong Kong was starting to feel like one big party!

When the show ended, they stayed outside on the deck. It was a bit chilly, but Alfie preferred to see all these amazing sights than to be warm right then.

"Your mom said you do gymnastics," Alfie said to Ying. "Is that where you were before you met us?"

"I don't *do* gymnastics," Ying said. "I *live* gymnastics. My parents' dream is to have a successful restaurant, and they're working hard to achieve their goal. My dream is to be a famous gymnast. And I have to work hard to make it happen."

"But food is fantastic!" exclaimed Emilia. "You get to be creative with it, it makes people happy, plus it can be totally delicious. What's not to like?"

"Tell that to my parents, and they'll love you forever," Ying said, laughing. "They're the ones who signed me up for gymnastics while they were busy working on building their business. But it turns out I'm really good at gymnastics. Now that I'm older and the restaurant is so close to opening, I'm sure they're going to want me to help out more."

"Can't you just tell them you'd rather do gymnastics?" Alfie asked.

"They're my parents. I can't disrespect them," Ying said simply. "I want the restaurant to be a success and for my parents to be happy. But I also want them to really care about what I want to do. Maybe now that you two are here you can be my backup, help me out in case I have to stay late at the gym."

The ferry finally arrived at the dock. Uncle Wu led the way down the promenade through the crowds of people—and there were thousands of people, shoulder-to-shoulder, waiting for the parade to begin. The family found a spot and they all squeezed together, Alfie taking care that Emilia was right next to him.

"Here it comes!" Ying said over the noise of the crowd, who were all cheering and clapping along with the music that came from the speakers and the parade that was making its way toward them.

Parts of the parade were like the ones back home—

floats carrying musicians, people dressed in costumes dancing, giant inflatable characters and animals floating overhead. There were also ornate paper dragons held up on sticks and worked by several people, weaving and diving and slithering down the street. Alfie could see two people inside a lion costume, dancing an elaborate, athletic dance as they went by, which Ying paid particularly close attention to.

Once the parade ended, Ying said, "Now the real show begins."

"There's more?" Emilia asked.

"Lots!"

They moved a bit closer to the water along with the crowd and positioned themselves in a tight little spot on the edge of the harbor.

"Fireworks next," Aunt Chan said. "Watch—they'll come from the boats."

"The Chinese invented fireworks, you know," Ying told them. "Like, thousands of years ago."

The first boom startled Alfie and Emilia. Alfie felt it in his chest. After an initial yelp from the crowd, everything went quiet, all faces looking upward. Suddenly, a white starburst filled the sky. The crowd cheered. The next round came quickly after that—several fireworks at a time, in all colors, sparkling and spiraling, going across the length of the harbor from boats moored in the water. From Kowloon they could see where they'd come from on Hong Kong Island, and they could see the island's skyscrapers and shiny glass buildings, all brightly lit up on the inside and outside, thanks to the fireworks reflecting off the glass. Alfie and Emilia stood transfixed as they watched the explosion of colors and shapes. It was like any Fourth of July they'd ever seen—times ten.

Once the evening's festivities ended, they made the trek back across the harbor. This time they decided to sit inside the ferry where it was warm. Everyone was quiet on the short ride back, tired from all the excitement.

When they got off the ferry, the extended family made their way home, and Alfie and Emilia followed Ying and her parents through the city streets to their apartment building. When they arrived inside the doors of their tenth-floor apartment, Alfie was almost too tired to take it all in. He noticed that it was small and clean and tidy.

Emilia was sharing Ying's room, and Alfie had his own small room next to them. Just as Alfie was about to get into bed, Ying stuck her head through the doorway.

"One last thing," she said. "Whatever you do, don't get up early. Sleep in late."

"Okay. But why?" Alfie asked.

"Bad luck for the elders if you get up early on the first day of the new year. Sleeping in means they'll have a long life, plus no trouble in the new year."

When Alfie finally turned out the lights and pulled up the covers, he felt relaxed and happy, ready for a new adventure. He was already having an amazing time and he didn't even have to worry about finding somewhere to stay or trying to find a way to feed himself and his sister. This time, things were going to be easier.

Chapter 6

Alfie had no problem sleeping in the next morning. He hadn't realized how exhausted he was from yesterday's activities.

It was quiet as he headed to the shared bathroom. As he tiptoed passed Ying and Emilia's room, he saw the door was open a crack. Emilia was alone, sitting on her bed and flipping through a magazine.

"Hey," Alfie said, sticking his head through the door. "What're you doing?"

"Looking at the Hong Kong version of *People* magazine," Emilia said. She tossed the magazine on the bed.

"Where's Ying?" Alfie asked as he stepped into the room.

Emilia picked up a piece of paper and showed it to Alfie.

Gone to gym. Shhh! Don't tell Mother and Father!

"I guess that means she got up early," Alfie said.

"I know," Emilia agreed. "Let's just hope they don't find out."

After they got dressed, Alfie and Emilia went into the living room. A few minutes later, Aunt Chan and Uncle Wu emerged from their room.

"You two slept in quite late!" Aunt Chan said, looking pleased.

Alfie was pretty sure that this was the first time in history he'd been praised for sleeping in. He definitely liked it here.

"Now let's see about these clothes," Aunt Chan said. They wore the same clothes as yesterday. It was all they had. They had told Ying and her parents there was some suitcase mix-up at the train station, and although they were a bit puzzled, they seemed to believe it. "You came to Hong Kong at the best time. Since it's New Year's Day, everyone gets new clothes. Come look!"

Emilia raced across the room when she saw what Aunt Chan was pointing to. Laid out on the table were clothes for them both—black cotton pants, billowy shirts, shoes, and overcoats.

"Oh my gosh, thank you!" Emilia said, holding a red embroidered top up to her shoulders. "It's so pretty! Alfie, what do you think?"

"It looks good," Alfie said. It made him happy to see his sister so excited. "Thank you—it's so nice of you to do this, but I think it's too much." There looked to be at least a week's worth of clothes for each of them.

"Nonsense," Uncle Wu said. "Please, you must accept it. It's tradition, and besides, it's part of your experience here in Hong Kong."

"Thank you, thank you!" Emilia said again, holding up another shirt to her shoulders.

"You're very welcome," Aunt Chan said. "Uncle Wu and I are going to the restaurant for the afternoon. There are some deliveries and other business we need to be there for. Ying will take you out for lunch and a bit of sightseeing."

Luckily, Aunt Chan and Uncle Wu left without asking about Ying. They must have assumed she was being good about sleeping in. She came home not five minutes after her parents had left.

"Hello!" she said, standing in the front hall. "Get your coats—we're going out."

The streets were still bustling with celebrations for the Spring Festival, which Ying explained would continue for the next six days. They passed one parade—not as big as last night's but still spectacular, with brightly colored costumes, beating drums, and stilt walkers—and locals and tourists shopped at the many little stores selling Spring Festival essentials like toy dragons, paper lanterns, and fried sesame-seed balls, among other treats.

Ying, Alfie, and Emilia took a boat across the harbor again but without all the fireworks and music. Once they got off the boat they walked through the city to Temple Street, where Ying said some of the best food in Hong Kong was served. Right there on the street, hot dishes were cooked up and served fresh—everything from noodles and broth to beef with oyster sauce prepared in well-used pots that looked like they'd been cooking up food for centuries. Canopies hung at uneven angles above the stalls, and many of the menus were handwritten on cardboard signs. Lots of people sat at the tables that lined the street, but some took their food and ate as they walked.

"In Hong Kong you can get any kind of food you want," Ying said. "Italian, French, Thai, you name it. People take food very seriously here. But on Temple Street, it's strictly Chinese and Hong Kong food. What do you feel like eating?" Smoke and steam filled the air—a mix of sweetness with a dash of heat.

"Alfie, look!" Emilia said, pointing. "Chickens' feet!"

"A Hong Kong classic," Ying said.

"Where's the rest of the chicken?" Emilia asked, looking a bit worried.

Ying smiled. "I'm sure it's around here somewhere. We don't waste food—everything gets eaten. You'll see."

"I don't think I'm brave enough to try chickens' feet," Emilia said, shaking her head.

"I am," Alfie said, with a smile.

"They're good," Ying said. "Just don't eat the nails."

"Ew!" Emilia said.

Ying laughed. "Just kidding. Well, you shouldn't eat them, but they'll cut them off for you. Hi, Mrs. Suen," she said to a woman at one of the stalls.

"Hello, Ying." She smiled back. "How's the restaurant opening going?"

"Fine," Ying said. "We open in a couple days. Mother and Father are there now, getting everything ready."

"We miss you down here," she said. "Tell your parents we said hello."

"I will," Ying said. "We used to have the stall right next to her," she explained to Alfie and Emilia.

"You call this *wan zai chi*?" snapped a woman at a nearby stall. She was short and wore a bright orange embroidered coat that reached down to her knees. Her black hair was cut in a sharp bob, and she wore serious-looking glasses. "There are hardly any mushrooms and this pork is barely shredded."

The woman handed the bowl back to the man at the stall and turned to leave. Unfortunately, she turned right into Ying.

"I'm sorry," Ying said, flustered. She looked at the

woman and said, "Um, hello, Mrs. Liu."

The woman furrowed her brow. "Have we met?"

"No, but I think you're coming to my family's restaurant soon. The Golden Lion?" Ying said nervously.

Mrs. Liu nodded. "Ah, yes. The new place on Hong Kong Island. The food at your family's stall was absolutely delicious. I wonder if you'll be able to achieve the same results at a restaurant."

With that, Mrs. Liu turned and headed down the street.

"And that," Ying said, "is Mrs. Liu. Maybe I shouldn't have said anything to her, but she made me nervous."

"You didn't say anything bad," Emilia said.

"The *wan zai chi* she just gave back is one of the best on all of Temple Street. I told you—she's very hard to please." Ying sighed. "Oh well. Let's go down here for the chickens' feet. You're going to love this."

Ying ordered up a bowl for Alfie, then got rib eye in sauce for herself. From a nearby stall, Emilia got pan-fried oyster cakes that looked a lot like the scallion pancakes they'd eaten with Zia Donatella. Once they all had their food, they went to find a place to sit. They found a table with three empty chairs. An elderly man sat in a fourth chair slurping noodles. Ying asked if they could share the table, and he nodded.

Alfie used his fingers to pick up a chicken's foot, which had been cooked in ginger, garlic, black-bean sauce, and soy sauce. He held it out to Emilia. "Wanna try?"

She shook her head. "No, thank you." Alfie could tell

she was trying to be nice in front of Ying and not say how gross she thought the food looked.

"Emilia, come on," he said. Zia Donatella didn't send them on these travels so that they could stick with what was comfortable.

"We should all share," Ying said. "The beef is so tender and the sauce is perfect. And I've never had the oyster cakes from that stall. Don't be shy, Emilia."

"I'm not," she said, but she looked skeptical.

"Remember the frogs' legs in Paris?" Alfie reminded her. "You liked those."

"True," Emilia said. She gingerly picked up a chicken's foot and held it away from her as if it might suddenly claw her.

"Is there a special way to eat this?" Emilia asked.

"Chickens' feet are all about the skin," Ying said. "It's crispy, so you chew it off with your teeth. Then you suck on the bones because there's lots of flavor in them. Spit out the bones, and place them on the side of the plate. It's

not the easiest thing to eat," she said, "but it's fun."

"Well," Alfie said, "the best part of fried chicken is the skin. I guess this is sort of the same thing."

"So dig in!" Ying said.

Alfie took a bite—as much as he could with the bones. It tasted a bit sweet and salty. He chewed the skin and then sucked on the boney bits, eventually spitting them out onto the side of his plate.

Emilia nibbled on hers, trying to delicately get the skin off and take the bone from her mouth. Ying said, "Face it—you can't be graceful eating chickens' feet."

Emilia laughed at herself and then attacked the chicken's foot again. "My friends will never believe I ate this," she said. "And that I actually liked it."

They shared the other dishes as well. The beef with sauce and vegetables required the use of chopsticks, which were still really hard for Alfie and Emilia to use. Alfie managed to get one chunk of beef into his mouth, but his second attempt fell out of the chopsticks. The meat was delicate and tender, and his stomach begged him to capture another chunk on his chopsticks, but he couldn't manage it. Luckily the oyster cakes—which were thin and crispy—could be eaten with his hands. He could taste the oyster but also scallions and parsley, reminding him of Zia's pancakes.

Once they'd finished, Alfie joked that it was "not that adventurous."

"He's just trying to show off," Emilia said.

"If that's the way you feel, I'll find you something that some Chinese people won't eat," Ying said.

"I can eat anything," Alfie said.

"I'll hold you to it," Ying said.

He had no doubt that she would.

Chapter 7

The next morning, they were up early—quite the difference from yesterday when they got to sleep in late.

"So," Uncle Wu said as they all cleared the breakfast table, "who wants to go visit Sai Kung with Ying? It's got some of the best fishing—and fishermen—in the city."

"And who wants to join us at the restaurant?" Aunt Chan asked. "We're going to make noodles and dumplings today."

"I'll go to Sai Kung," Alfie said. "It's probably a lot different than fishing at home."

"And I want to learn how to make noodles and dumplings," said Emilia. "Zia will be so excited to hear about that when we get home."

Alfie and Emilia looked at each other. They'd been so busy since they arrived in Hong Kong that they hadn't really thought about home. Of course they missed Mom, Dad, and Zia, but they knew from their other adventures that everything at home would be okay.

"Ying, you can take Alfie to Sai Kung, and Emilia can come with us," Aunt Chan said with a smile.

"What?" Ying asked sharply. "I showed them around yesterday. I want to spend the day at the gymnastics studio."

"Now, Ying," her mother replied, "if Alfie wants to go fishing, as a gracious host you should accompany him."

"I suppose so," Ying said with a roll of her eyes. "But I need time at the gym."

"I understand," Uncle Chan said, "but only once you're done showing Alfie around."

Ying let out a sigh. "Oh, all right, I'll get my coat."

Out on the streets, Ying's parents and Emilia headed

to the restaurant, and Alfie and Ying headed to the town of Sai Kung.

"It's about forty-five minutes away," Ying explained. "We just have to walk toward Wan Chai and get on the minibus."

"Minibus," Alfie repeated. "Got it." He always liked to know where things were and how to get to them, especially during their adventures. "Which area of town will we be in?"

"New Territories," she explained. "It's the largest of Hong Kong's districts, and it's also the most rural. There are lots of farms and small villages there."

Once they arrived at Wan Chai, they got on a red minibus. The bus took them through the tunnel under Victoria Harbor, through the city area of Kowloon with all its modern high-rise buildings, until they were in an area with green rolling hills and small farming towns. In less than an hour, they arrived at Sai Kung near the promenade.

Just over the promenade railing, boats rocked gently in the water, all crammed tightly together with old tires hanging on the sides to keep them from scraping one another. Most were painted green or blue, with weathered beach umbrellas shading the person sitting inside the boat. The boats were filled with containers of fish that Alfie didn't recognize, as well as bags of food, all lined up. The fish in the open containers were covered in water, and they were still alive. Some fishermen were descaling and gutting fish right there on the boat.

"It's like a floating fish market here," Ying explained. "They sell everything in their boats, and they sell to the public and local restaurants. As you can see, we take our fresh fish very seriously. There's Kang!"

Ying waved as they walked toward a small, older man with a weathered face and bright eyes. He waved back.

"Hello, Ying," the old man said. "How's the lion?"

"The Golden Lion? It's great. Our big opening is tomorrow," Ying said.

"Of course, I know that," Kang said. "I mean *your* lion."

A smile crept across Ying's face as she said, "Better than ever."

"Your lion?" Alfie asked.

"Oh, it's just—nothing," Ying said quickly. "Alfie, this is Kang. He is the best fisherman in Hong Kong. Father plans on making the extra trip out here for our fish each morning, even though the Aberdeen market is closer. When you know the city's best fisherman, you have to go to him," she said.

"The fish love me. I can't help but catch them. Are you ready to be a fisherman today?" he asked Alfie.

"Definitely," Alfie said.

"Great," Ying said. "Have fun."

"You're not coming fishing with us?" Alfie asked.

"I need to get to the gym," she said. "I can come back and get you in a couple hours if you're not comfortable going back on your own, but it's really easy. Just take the minibus back, and I'll write down directions from the station."

Alfie felt a bit nervous. He was good with getting around, but this city was huge. It was definitely intimidating.

When he didn't respond right away, Ying said, "If you're scared, I'll come back and get you. It's not a problem."

"I'm not scared," Alfie said, trying to sound confident. It would be easier for Ying to come back and get him, but he didn't want her to think he wasn't capable of finding his way back. "I can do it. Just write down good directions."

"Okay, great," Ying said. She dug a piece of paper and a pencil out of her bag. "Go straight back to the restaurant. I should be there by the time you come back."

Alfie wasn't totally comfortable about being part of Ying's scheme, especially when her parents already were stressed about the restaurant opening. He didn't promise her anything, just took the directions and said, "Thanks."

"Good luck!" she called, waving as she walked away.

"Ready?" Kang asked. "The fish are waiting."

Chapter 8

Kang led Alfie to a small boat docked near the harbor. Being outside the city, Alfie realized how quiet the world was here, with just the sound of water lapping up to the harbor walls. He could no longer see the big city buildings. Instead, they were surrounded by green hills; off in the distance, small islands dotted the landscape.

"Fishing is easy as long as you remember one thing," Kang said as he stepped gently into the boat.

Alfie followed him in, careful to keep steady in the rocking waters. "What's that?"

Kang sat on the seat and started the engine, which sputtered with a puff of exhaust. "It's all in your energy.

The fish can feel it. They're attracted to it. If you are too fidgety, they stay away. So," he said, "stay calm."

Which seemed easy to do out on the water, away from the chaos of the city. All Alfie could hear was the slow engine of the boat and the water moving around them.

Kang showed Alfie how to bait the hook with his special blend of bloodworm and his secret weapon, which he said he couldn't tell anyone. "Not even my wife," he said.

The bloodworm looked about how Alfie expected— long, slimy, and a rusty red color. It was alive and squirmy as he tried to hook it onto his line. Once he managed to get it on, Kang showed him how to toss out his line.

"Look out at the water," he said, "and let the fish tell you where to throw your line."

Alfie thought it was all slightly strange, but he was willing to give it a try. So he looked out at the water, saw a spot he thought might be good (but really had no idea), and threw out his line the way Kang showed him.

"Very nice," Kang said. He sat down on the bench and tossed his line out with ease. "Now, we wait."

If someone had told him a week ago that he would enjoy sitting in a fishing boat in the cold with an old man being perfectly silent, he would have laughed. But there was something Alfie liked about fishing that morning. Something about the quiet of the shifting water, and knowing he was so close to the quick pace of the city but also very removed from it.

Suddenly, he felt a tug on his line.

"I got something!"

Alfie excitedly pulled back on the line. Kang scooted

over to him and put one hand on his shoulder and the other on the top of his hand, steadying him.

"If you get too excited, the fish will, too," Kang said. "Be calm, and he'll swim to you."

Alfie worried that the weight of the struggling fish would pull him into the water, but he used all his strength and tried his best to stay calm. Once he reeled the fish in and Kang helped put it in the bucket of water in the bottom of the boat, Alfie felt the full moment of success through patience.

"I did it," Alfie said as he tried to catch his breath from excitement and exertion. The fish was as big as his forearm! It was silver with brown spots and orange fins.

"Very good," Kang said, inspecting the fish. "That's a

beautiful cod. Have the family cook this up for you when you return to the restaurant. Eating what you catch is the best reward."

"Thanks," Alfie said, proud that he'd done it on his first try. He was a natural!

Kang and Alfie stayed out on the water for a while. They didn't catch any more fish, but that didn't matter to Alfie. He was glad he'd decided to join Kang rather than go to the restaurant.

Once they got back to the promenade, Kang scaled and gutted the fish, then put it in a plastic bag for Alfie.

"Thanks for showing me how to fish," Alfie said, taking the bag from Kang.

"Get that fish back as quickly as you can," Kang said. "The fresher the better!"

Alfie couldn't wait to taste it! He'd get back to the restaurant as soon as he could.

Chapter 9

The entire way back, Alfie had butterflies in his stomach, worried that he might get lost. Luckily, the directions and simple map that Ying had given him were very clear, and he only took one wrong turn and realized his mistake quickly. *Yep, my map-reading skills and sense of direction are pretty awesome,* Alfie thought as he turned the corner and saw the Golden Lion.

Although the restaurant would not open until tomorrow, it was a hive of activity. He saw Aunt Chan walk by, pan in hand, a look of concentration on her face. Alfie found Emilia by the aquarium, staring at the fish.

"What's wrong?" he asked.

"I got in trouble." She kept her eyes on the fish, tracing her finger over the glass.

"What'd you do?"

"I swept the floor," she said, her voice cracking a bit.

Alfie wanted to laugh, but his sister seemed so upset that he didn't dare. "I don't get it. Shouldn't you be thanked for that?"

"You'd think. I didn't know that sweeping during the Spring Festival is bad luck," Emilia explained. "It's like sweeping all the good luck right out the door. I was just trying to help out. Uncle Wu came running over, waving his hands for me to stop. When he told me, I was so embarrassed."

"You didn't know," Alfie said. He put his hand on her shoulder and gave it a squeeze. He hated seeing his sister upset.

"There you are!" Aunt Chan called to Alfie, coming out of the kitchen and wiping her hands on a towel. She forced a smile, but Alfie thought she looked tired and a bit worn out. "How was the fishing?"

"Great," Alfie said, holding up the bag. "I caught this."

"Well, congratulations! We should cook that up right away." Which was exactly what he wanted to do. He wanted to learn the best way to cook it and see how fish this fresh tasted. "Where's Ying?"

Alfie and Emilia looked nervously at each other—that was a tricky question.

"Uh . . . ," Alfie began. He looked to Emilia for help. "I thought . . ."

"She must be right behind you, right, Alfie?" Emilia looked at him hard, telling him with her eyes to just go with it.

"Well?" Aunt Chan asked.

When he didn't say anything, Aunt Chan folded her arms and said, "Did she leave you all the way out in Sai Kung?"

Uncle Wu walked out from the kitchen just then and said, "Alfie! You're back! Where is Ying?"

"I bet I know where she is," Aunt Chan said sharply.

"Ying didn't stay with you?" Uncle Wu asked Alfie.

Alfie hated ratting her out, but he didn't want to lie. "I told her it was okay. I knew I could get back on my own—it was easy."

"What are we going to do with that girl?" Aunt Chan said. "Her disobedience is going to jinx us."

"Now, now," Uncle Wu said.

"What if that Mrs. Liu shows up tomorrow? The first day of business—that'd be just our luck."

"She probably won't. Reviewers know businesses need a few days to settle in," Uncle Wu said. He looked to Alfie and Emilia. "For now, maybe I should take you two home. It's been a long day."

"Don't forget that the electrician is coming, and I need to pick up the tablecloths we ordered."

"Oh, that's right," Uncle Wu said.

"We can go back on our own," Alfie said. "If you could write down directions, that is. I'd like to learn the way."

"Well, I suppose you did make it on your own from Sai Kung, and the apartment isn't far from here," Uncle Wu said, thinking. "I'll give you the apartment keys. You're sure you'll be okay?"

"We'll be fine," Emilia said, suddenly stepping up. "I'd like to see more of the city by walking the streets, anyway."

"Are you absolutely sure?" Aunt Chan asked.

Alfie watched Emilia nod her head with total confidence, saying, "Yes, we're sure."

"And as for Ying," Aunt Chan said, "she had better be at the apartment when we get home tonight. "

Uncle Wu wrote down directions—it wasn't a far walk, maybe fifteen minutes—and Aunt Chan handed her cell phone to Emilia. "Take this, in case you get lost or we need to get in touch with you."

As soon as they left the restaurant, Emilia said, "We have to warn Ying."

"How are we going to warn her?" Alfie said. "We don't

even know where she is. Wait," he said, seeing a look in his sister's eyes. "Do you know where she is?"

"She's at the gym," Emilia said.

"I figured that," Alfie said. "But do you know how to get there?"

"She gave me directions, just in case."

"Ying's already in trouble, and now we're going to be in trouble."

"She's just doing what she loves," Emilia said. "I think it's cool, and I like her."

"I like her, too, but she's stressing out her parents. Why can't she just, like, *behave*?"

"You mean like you always do?" Emilia said.

"I'm just saying," Alfie said, slightly embarrassed.

After a couple more turns, they came to a sign that had both Chinese characters and English words. WEI'S SCHOOL OF GYMNASTICS, MARTIAL ARTS, AND DANCE, it read. Alfie followed Emilia inside.

It was hard to believe that in a city so compact that

people literally lived on top of each other in high-rise apartments that there could be a space as huge as this.

WEI'S SCHOOL OF GYMNA[

The students looked like a bunch of bouncy balls. Everywhere Alfie looked, girls and boys sprang across mats, flipped over bars, and twisted through the air.

"There she is," Emilia said, pointing to the other side of the room.

Ying was off to the side, separated from the others and working privately with a coach and another girl. They were doing some sort of routine that looked almost like ballet. She and the girl dipped into a low, graceful slide before moving back up then twisting their bodies this way and that.

Alfie and Emilia watched for a few minutes as Ying and the girl worked on their moves with the coach. They'd never seen anything like it—a combination of dance and gymnastics and maybe even martial arts that was both graceful and powerful. The other girl lifted Ying almost to her shoulders, then gently set her down as they bent in a wavelike movement.

"I thought she was doing regular gymnastics," Emilia said. "This is amazing."

Alfie totally agreed. Their coach dismissed them, but Ying obviously wanted to run through the section again. She kept shaking her head as if she felt it could be done better. Alfie realized that he'd thought she was irresponsible because she never showed up on time; he'd thought she was lazy because she never wanted to help her parents. It turned out she'd been working hard all along—harder even than he'd worked at soccer, or anything else, really.

"Think we should go over to her and tell her she needs to go home?" Emilia asked.

"I'm afraid to interrupt her," Alfie said.

"Yeah. Me too."

Ying and her partner finally did stop. The coach gave them high fives.

"We'd better get her," Alfie said. "Otherwise she'll be here all night."

They walked across the gym toward Ying. When she saw them, a surprised look spread across her face.

"Ying, you're amazing!" Emilia said. "We had no idea."

"Thanks," she said. She stopped for a drink of water. "Wait—if the two of you are here, it must mean there's trouble at the restaurant."

"There is," Emilia said. "You'd better head home."

"Oh no. What happened?" Ying asked.

"Emilia swept the floors," Alfie said.

"And they know you left Alfie at Sai Kung," Emilia added.

Ying quickly pulled on her tracksuit. "We should go."

"And fast," Emilia said. They hurried out of the gym. "Your mom said you'd better be at the apartment when they get home, or else."

"Let's hope they've cooled off once they get there," Ying said.

They all hoped so, but Alfie had a feeling they wouldn't be so lucky.

Chapter 10

Aunt Chan and Uncle Wu had indeed cooled off by the time they got home—to the point of being cold. They looked tired and disappointed, and they barely spoke. Alfie felt a new pang of guilt, knowing that he and Emilia were a part of the reason their day had been tough.

The family ate an uncomfortably silent dinner of beef in a black-bean sauce. Aunt Chan and Uncle Wu also cooked Alfie's cod, which he was happy for even though he felt bad for what had happened. Alfie worked slowly with his chopsticks, careful not to drop the food—although he did, and often. His hand kept cramping from the effort. He remembered what Aunt Chan said about spearing his food, which his stomach begged him to do, but he knew better. The cod he managed to get to his mouth was delicate and flaky, and he wished for a fork so he could eat every last bite.

"As you know, the restaurant opens tomorrow," Uncle Wu said during dinner. "I didn't think I needed to remind anyone of that, but maybe I do." Ying lowered her head, and Alfie knew she really did feel bad about the day.

"As for you," Aunt Chan said, looking at Ying, "you're to be there at the restaurant all day. We need you to help, and you need to learn some responsibility."

"This means that tomorrow," Uncle Wu said, "you will not go to gymnastics."

"But, Father!"

The look he gave Ying made it clear he wouldn't be swayed. "It's just one day, and it's our most important day. Surely you can handle that without complaining."

"But, Father, you don't understand . . . ," Ying said.

"That's enough—any more and it will be more than just one day of no gymnastics."

"I can't believe he did that," Ying said later that evening as they sat in Ying and Emilia's room. A plate of almond cookies sat on the bed between them. "It'll be a disaster if I can't practice."

"What were you and that girl practicing, anyway?" Emilia asked.

Ying sat up straight and her eyes brightened. "That's the big thing I'm working on. Ju and I are rehearsing for a dance we'll do at the parade in four days."

"You get to march in the parade?" Emilia said.

"Not march," Ying said. "Dance. Well, acrobatic dance. Like martial arts meets gymnastics meets dance. Sort of."

"So that's what we saw you working on at the gym?" Emilia asked.

"It's actually kind of a big deal," Ying said, blushing slightly. "Ju and I were chosen as the junior dancers to perform. We're in a traditional Chinese costume. It's an elaborate lion and I'm in the front. I control its head and move its mouth and even its eyes. It's a tradition about scaring away evil spirits and bringing luck to the new year."

"Is *everything* done to bring luck?" Alfie asked.

"Well, you can never have too much of it, right?" Ying said. "Now you know why I've been so crazy. I'm really not always so sneaky, but Ju and I have extra rehearsals so it's been more than my regular gym time. I'm sorry I've put you in so many awkward situations."

"It's okay," Emilia said. "You're just trying to do something you love and that will make your parents proud."

"Exactly," Ying said. "I really do want to make them proud of me. Hopefully once they see me in the parade they'll understand."

"Just remember what your dad said," Alfie reminded her.

Ying snapped another almond cookie in two. "Father's bark is worse than his bite," she said.

Alfie helped himself to another cookie and let himself believe that everything would be okay.

Chapter 11

The next morning, Aunt Chan and Uncle Wu woke everyone up early for a surprise.

"This is a tradition in Hong Kong," Uncle Wu said. "And we think it's important to do with the restaurant opening today."

"It's a big day for all of us," Aunt Chan said. "We need lots of good luck!"

The surprise was a trip to a temple in a small village just a short bus ride from the apartment. They walked through a courtyard packed with people and in the center of the crowd stood a large tree glowing bright with orange balls and red ribbons. As they got closer,

Alfie realized the balls were actually oranges.

"There aren't many places left that still allow you to toss oranges into the trees," Uncle Wu explained. "Most use sticks—easier on the tree since they're not as heavy. But here they still keep up the old tradition. Write down a wish for the new year." Uncle Wu handed everyone a red piece of paper with a hole punched in the top. "Make it a good one, something special."

Ying and Aunt Chan were already bent over the small folding table busily writing on their pieces of paper. Alfie thought carefully about what to write as he waited for a pen.

"There," Aunt Chan said, holding up her card. She showed it to Alfie.

"It's okay if I see?" he asked. "At home it's bad luck to tell your wish, like when you blow out your birthday candles or toss a coin into a fountain."

Aunt Chan smiled. "Go ahead."

May our restaurant thrive and prosper.

"Now it's your turn," Aunt Chan said.

Alfie thought carefully before writing his wish. Finally, he wrote: *May I always travel and learn about other places.*

Once everyone had a wish written and tied to an orange, it was time to toss them onto the tree.

"The goal is to hook it over a branch," Ying explained. "Otherwise it's—"

"Bad luck?" Alfie guessed.

Ying smiled. "Exactly."

With a gentle underhand toss, Alfie's orange flew high up the side of the tree, missing branches as it went. He held his breath as it came back down and finally caught a branch. The orange swung for a moment before coming to a stop.

"Perfect!" Ying said.

Emilia was next. On her piece of paper she wrote, *My wish is to always be brave enough to try new things.* She threw hers overhand, and her orange easily wrapped

around a branch high up the tree.

"Nicely done!" Aunt Chan told her. "High branches are extra lucky."

Aunt Chan and Uncle Wu flung their oranges up and both caught branches. Now it was Ying's turn.

"Ying, did you write a good wish?" Uncle Wu asked.

"Very good."

"Something for the family?"

"Of course," Ying said with a determined look in her eyes. "Watch this." She turned her back to the tree and just as she tossed the orange backward over her head, her mother yelled, "Ying, no!" The orange sailed over Ying's head toward the tree. It smacked a branch, jiggled several other oranges, and fell to the ground with a *thunk*.

Aunt Chan gasped. Uncle Wu lowered his head. Ying said, "Whoops."

"I can't believe it," Aunt Chan said. "The bad luck just keeps coming."

"I wish you would take these things seriously," Uncle Wu said to Ying.

"I do," she said. "I just thought—I don't know . . ."

"Exactly," Uncle Wu said. "You didn't think."

"It won't hurt the restaurant," she said. "It was a wish for myself."

"For yourself?" Aunt Chan said. "You're supposed to be thinking about the family, and the family is the restaurant."

From the look on her face and her posture, Alfie could tell that Ying regretted carelessly tossing her orange. If she had wished to do well in the parade, and she believed

in the wishing tree, then she probably believed her dance was doomed.

"Maybe we should make one more stop," Aunt Chan said. "I know there's a lot to do to prepare the restaurant for opening but . . . this is important."

She looked to Uncle Wu, who seemed to know what she was thinking. He nodded yes. "If one Buddha is good, then ten thousand should be even better." He looked to Alfie and Emilia. "What do you think? Would you like to see them?"

Alfie and Emilia looked at each other and then at Ying. If going to see the Buddhas meant good luck and it would make Aunt Chan and Uncle Wu happy, then of course they'd go. "Yes," they replied together.

Knowing Ying felt terrible about the wishing tree, Alfie and Emilia stayed close to her on the way to the temple. None of them spoke, and it was a quiet bus ride.

Alfie didn't actually believe there would be ten thousand Buddhas in one place. It seemed impossible.

But he was starting to learn that Hong Kong was full of surprises.

"We're headed to the Ten Thousand Buddhas Monastery, or Man Fat Tsz," Uncle Wu explained as the bus made its way up a hill. "It's one of Hong Kong's most famous Buddhist temples, and one of its most popular tourist attractions."

When they arrived at the temple, they started up the steps—four hundred, the sign said—on a narrow stone path with a low red wall. Propped along the wall were bronze Buddha statues, all seated, all life-size, and each with a different expression on its face. It went on and on, but Alfie didn't mind the climb—he was too busy looking at the faces: one played a flute, another had a long, thin beard; some were bald, some had curly hair; one was screaming, one was laughing, and another looked worried. It was incredible.

As they walked farther into the grounds, they realized that there weren't really ten thousand Buddhas in this place—there were more.

The walls inside the temple were lined top to bottom with shelves filled with miniature Buddhas. There had to be thousands in that room alone. Back outside on the grounds, there was one giant golden Buddha who had over a thousand arms. One rode on top of a blue dragon-like creature, another sat atop some serpent-like creature. It really was one of the most amazing things Alfie had ever seen.

They all climbed to the top of the nine-floor pagoda to take in the view of the mountains behind them and the city below them.

"This has been amazing," Alfie said. "Thank you for showing it to us."

"Now, who feels like opening a restaurant?" Uncle Wu said. They all started back down the hill for the Golden Lion. Alfie hoped that all they'd done and seen this morning would help make it the best opening in restaurant history.

Chapter 12

When they got to the Golden Lion, everyone snapped into action. Aunt Chan and Uncle Wu asked the chef and waiters to get the kitchen ready. And they asked Ying, Alfie, and Emilia to help as well. Alfie was in charge of folding the napkins and Emilia helped with chopping vegetables. Aunt Chan told Ying she had to wipe down the tables. Alfie hadn't seen her work so quickly since he and Emilia arrived. She kept checking the clock above the stove, and Alfie knew she was thinking about rehearsing her performance.

Finally, everything was set and it was time. Aunt Chan flipped the switch on the sign outside, and Uncle

Wu unlocked and opened the front door. "We're open!" they said.

"Congratulations!" The family members who had been at dinner the night of Alfie and Emilia's arrival streamed into the restaurant. There were hugs and handshakes, and then the waiter showed everyone to a table in the middle of the restaurant.

But then they waited.

"It's still a bit early in the lunch hour," Uncle Wu said to Aunt Chan. "They'll come. I know it."

"Yes, yes," Aunt Chan said, with a nervous look on her face.

Just as Alfie started to think that maybe Emilia's sweeping and Ying's wishing-tree miss might have had some effect on the restaurant, two customers walked in.

"Welcome!" Aunt Chan said excitedly, rushing over to them. "Let me show you to a table. We'll bring out some tea right away."

The waiter took over from Aunt Chan and handed the couple menus. Soon, there was a steady stream of customers. Alfie helped clear tables and Emilia refilled water glasses.

Once the last lunch customer had been served, Aunt Chan said she was going to run out to the market to pick up some extra vegetables for dinner. "I have a feeling Mrs. Liu is coming tonight, so I want to make sure we're well stocked."

"Everything is under control here," Uncle Wu said. "You go on."

Apparently Ying saw this as an opportunity as well.

"Hey, Alfie," she whispered. She stood just inside the back door, motioning for Alfie to follow her. "Listen," she said. "I want to head out for rehearsal as soon as I can. Will you cover for me?"

"Your parents want you here," he said.

"I know," she said, "but lunch is over, and Mother is gone. And the cook and the waiter are still here. I'll be back long before dinner."

He knew how important her lion dance was—he could see it when he watched her rehearse with Ju—but the restaurant was important to her parents, and he didn't think she should do anything to upset them.

Apparently Ying could see the hesitation in his eyes. "Alfie . . ."

"I'll help you." Emilia had appeared from behind them. "Go on. I'll cover for you."

"Thank you, Emilia!" Ying said. "You're a lifesaver."

Ying was out the door before Alfie could speak another word.

"I don't know, Emilia," Alfie said, "this doesn't feel right to me."

"You're becoming as superstitious as the rest of them," Emilia said.

Just as the last lunch customer left and Ying was probably walking through the gym doors, Uncle Wu raced into the kitchen, "She's here! Mrs. Liu is here!"

"Wait, seriously?" Alfie said. "Why has she shown up so late?" Maybe this was one of her ways of testing restaurants.

The cook and waiter were about to leave. Uncle Wu turned to them and said, "With Aunt Chan gone, I'll need you to stay and help. We need to make a good impression."

"It's going to be okay," Emilia said coolly. "Alfie and I can help as well."

Uncle Wu nodded and looked around. "Where is Ying?"

"Well," Emilia began. "Um . . ."

Uncle Wu turned to Emilia and said, "She didn't leave, did she?" Emilia and Alfie stayed silent. "Are you telling me she left to go to the gym?" He shook his head. "That girl. If her mother was here . . ."

"We need to worry about Mrs. Liu right now," Emilia said. Alfie was glad she took the attention off Ying.

"You're right," Uncle Wu said. "I'm angry with Ying, but the most important thing now is looking after Mrs. Liu."

Mrs. Liu sat primly in the center of the restaurant, eyeing every inch of the space around her. A notebook and pen sat on the table in front of her.

"Welcome to the Golden Lion," Uncle Wu said, approaching her table with a menu. "I hope you are well— we have some tea for you on its way."

"Yes, I have been waiting," Mrs. Liu said.

The waiter rushed out of the kitchen with a pot and teacup on a tray, which he set down on the table with trembling hands. Uncle Wu poured tea into the cup.

"Thank you," Mrs. Liu said. She took a sip and pursed her lips. "Not very hot, is it?"

"Oh, I'm so sorry," Uncle Wu said. "We will get you another." The waiter dashed back into the kitchen.

"Let me tell you about our dishes," Uncle Wu said with a smile. "All of our fish was caught just this morning. We have a wonderful grouper prepared with chili and soy sauce, a lightly fried squid seasoned with just a little salt and pepper, and mantis shrimp cooked with a hint of chili. Please take your time to look over the menu—"

"I'll start with hot-and-sour cabbage and an order of shrimp dumplings with no pork."

"Wonderful," Uncle Wu said. "We'll get that started while you look at the rest of this—"

"No, I know what I want." Looking at the menu, she said, "Bring me an order of your stir-fried grouper filet. The beef with oyster sauce. And then . . ." She closed the menu, pulled off her glasses and looked thoughtfully at Uncle Wu. "I'm in the mood for razor clams. I know they're not on the menu, but I'd love some. Feel free to cook them however you'd like." She smiled and handed the menu back to Uncle Wu.

From the kitchen Alfie could see the panic in Uncle Wu's eyes. But unfazed, he said, "Of course. Whatever you want. Your tea will be right out."

"I hope so," Mrs. Liu replied. She dusted an invisible spot on the table.

Uncle Wu rushed into the kitchen. "I can't believe the biggest meal of our lives is upon us and none of my family is here," Uncle Wu said, looking around the kitchen. "I can't leave the restaurant. And I don't want to send the cook or waiter to go get razor clams—that will just make it look like we're unprepared."

"We're here," Alfie said. "Let us help."

"I'm going to have to see if Aunt Chan can go get some razor clams," Uncle Wu said with a sigh. He grabbed the phone on the wall and dialed. After listening for a moment, he slowly hung up. "Straight to voice mail.

This is a disaster!" He looked at everyone in the kitchen. "Emilia, can you help the cook and waiter with whatever they need?"

"Of course," she said.

"And Alfie," Uncle Wu said. He looked at Alfie carefully, closely. "The biggest task of all. I know we can get some razor clams at the Aberdeen Fish Market. Will you go get them for me?"

"Yes," Alfie said without a second thought, even though he had no idea where the market was or what razor clams looked like.

"Here's money for a cab," Uncle Wu said, digging cash out of his pocket. "Tell the driver where you want to go and ask him to wait for you. It'll cost extra, but it's no problem. Then race in and get those clams—get ten of them, just in case. Can you do this?"

"Yes, I can," Alfie said, hoping it was true.

"Okay," Uncle Wu said. "Off you go."

Chapter 13

In just ten minutes the cab flew across Hong Kong
Island to the south side where the city's largest market,
Aberdeen Fish Market, was located. When they pulled up
Alfie asked the driver to wait for him, just as Uncle Wu
had instructed.

The market was a huge warehouse right on the edge
of the water. Boats could easily unload their day's catches
and haul them into the open space, where buyers walked
down the wet cement floors and inspected all kinds
of freshly caught fish laid out in plastic buckets. Alfie
wasn't sure where to begin—he sped down one aisle, then
another, looking for what might be razor clams. Through

the wide open doors he saw a boat pull up to the dock, and decided to run out and see what that fisherman had—and if he could get it fresh off the boat.

At Sai Kung he got a feeling of peaceful, rural fishing; here it was the noise of motorboats and people hauling gear and yelling out prices. The chaos made Alfie feel the pressure to hurry up and pick something.

One fisherman was an elderly man in a green bamboo hat sitting patiently in his boat, and something about him relaxed Alfie.

"Do you need fresh fish?" the man asked as Alfie approached him.

"The freshest," Alfie said. "Do you have any razor clams?"

The man nodded. "I do. Caught some this morning. But I just now got back from catching scallops. Freshest in the entire market. They're still alive in their shells. See?" He showed Alfie the blue plastic bucket the scallops were in.

The shells were like what Alfie might find on a beach—white and fan-shaped. He looked more closely at the barely open shell. "What are the bright blue circles?" Alfie asked.

"The eyes," the man said. "Haven't you ever seen fresh scallops before?"

Alfie raised his eyebrows. "No."

"Is this for your family?" the man asked.

"Family restaurant," Alfie said. "But it's for this one very particular customer."

"I see," the man said. "Well, I can sell you the clams and the scallops if you like."

Alfie counted the money Uncle Wu had given him. With the cab fare back, he realized could only afford one. When he told the fisherman this, the man said, "They're both good. You don't need to worry about that. How picky is this customer?"

"The pickiest, toughest eater ever," Alfie said.

"A true Hong Kong diner can tell the difference

between just-caught and hours-ago-caught seafood. We like our seafood fresh here. Otherwise, what's the point of living on the water?"

Alfie pictured Mrs. Liu's face, scolding Uncle Wu for either serving hours-old seafood if Alfie bought the clams, or for not giving the customer what she wanted if he bought the extremely fresh scallops. He didn't know what to do, but he knew he had to make a decision, and quickly.

He pointed to the seafood he thought would most impress Mrs. Liu. "I'll take those, please," he said.

The man nodded and bagged them up. Alfie handed over the money.

"Thanks so much!" Alfie said as he turned to leave. "You may have just saved a restaurant!"

The cab came to a screeching halt outside the Golden Lion. Before he went inside, Alfie took deep breaths to calm down. He went around to the back door and entered the kitchen.

"Just in time," Uncle Wu said to Alfie as he put the bag on the counter. "The other dishes will be ready in a minute."

Emilia raced over to him. "Did you get the razor clams?"

Alfie didn't answer, butterflies filling his stomach as Uncle Wu looked into the bag.

"What is this?" Uncle Wu said. He held the seafood Alfie had scored in his hand. "These are scallops. She specifically said razor clams."

"Alfie," Emilia began, looking at the scallops then back at him. To Uncle Wu she said, "Maybe he didn't know the difference."

"No, listen," Alfie said. Suddenly his confidence disappeared. "The fisherman just caught these. He said they'd be fresher than the clams." Uncle Wu and Emilia stood staring at him with disbelieving eyes. "She's going to love them—more than the razor clams. I'm sure of it," he added, although he had no idea. Alfie realized he'd taken a huge risk.

Uncle Wu looked around the kitchen as if a better answer might present itself. But none did. "Okay. They only take a few minutes to cook. I'll just sear them with a bit of garlic and ginger." He ran his hand over his face. "I'll explain to Mrs. Liu that we just got this in and didn't want to serve it to anyone but her. Hopefully she'll be okay with it."

Uncle Wu got to work on the scallops. Alfie and Emilia watched as he used a dull straight knife to pop open each shell, then ran that knife along the bottom of the scallop to release it. It was covered with a bunch of slimy stuff, which Uncle Wu scraped and peeled away. He sautéed the scallops with the other ingredients, and when he was satisfied that they were perfectly cooked, the waiter helped him carry all three entrées out to Mrs. Liu. They carefully set the dishes in front of her on the table.

"I have a special surprise for you," Uncle Wu said. "We were lucky enough to get these fresh scallops just now from the market. These were caught less than an hour ago, and were alive just minutes ago. You won't find a fish more beautiful than this in all of Hong Kong."

"Scallops?" Mrs. Liu looked at the plate suspiciously. "What about my razor clams? I asked specifically for that."

"Yes, I understand," Uncle Wu said. "I didn't think you'd care for them—they were caught this morning."

"I see," Mrs. Liu said. "So you know what I want more than I do? I guess I'll just have to taste what you've served here. Thank you," she added curtly. Uncle Wu nodded and quietly stepped away.

Everyone watched anxiously from the kitchen as she took a bite of the scallop dish, and then another. She scribbled a note in her notebook then took another bite. She tasted the other dishes as well, adding more notes to her notebook. Suddenly she motioned toward the back and Uncle Wu went right over. Alfie and Emilia watched as Uncle Wu bowed his head and took the half-eaten plates of food away.

"What'd she say?" Emilia asked as he came through the kitchen.

His face looked stricken. "She said she was finished."

He put the plates of food on the counter.

They all guessed what that meant: Mrs. Liu was unhappy with the food and would surely write a negative review. Alfie felt sick to his stomach.

"Hello, I'm back," a voice called. They turned to see Aunt Chan come in through the back entrance with bags full of fresh produce. "Did I miss anything?"

Uncle Wu turned ash white. "Mrs. Liu—she's just finishing her meal."

Aunt Chan froze. "She's here? Why didn't you call me? How is it going? Is she pleased with her meal?"

Uncle Wu's slumped shoulders said it all. He sighed and said, "I'm afraid not. She requested razor clams—"

"Razor clams?" Aunt Chan said. "Those aren't on the menu. Did you go to the market to get some?"

It wasn't until now that Alfie started to think that maybe these adventures Zia sent them on were too tough on his heart. It was pounding so hard he was sure it was going to burst out of his chest.

"It's my fault," Alfie said. "I didn't get the right—"

"It doesn't matter," Uncle Wu said. "She barely ate any of the dishes. I can only assume what she thought of them."

Everyone stood in silence, the realization of what might happen to the restaurant washing over them. It was at that exact moment that Ying walked into the kitchen.

"Hey, everyone!" she said, all cheerful. "I'm just finishing in the pantry. Anyone need any help with anything?"

"Ying," Uncle Wu said, "where have you been?"

Ying's eyes darted between Alfie and Emilia, but there was no look Alfie could give her that could explain what had happened that day.

"I was—I stepped outside for a little bit," she said. "To get some air."

"Where exactly were you?" Aunt Chan asked sternly.

Ying's head dropped. "I was at the gym."

Aunt Chan stiffened her back. "Just what I thought.

That is absolutely it. You are done with that gym. No more gymnastics."

"But, Mother!"

"You have had plenty of chances," Aunt Chan said. "And still you disobey us. If you had been here you could have helped."

"What happened?" Ying asked.

"The fact that you do not know tells us that you don't care," Aunt Chan said.

"Mother, that's not true," Ying said desperately. She looked to Uncle Wu and said, "Father . . ." Her voice trailed off. She looked like she was about to cry. Alfie felt miserable.

Why hadn't he followed the directions given to him? He felt as horrible as Ying did.

Chapter 14

The work at the restaurant over the next few days was just that—all work. There were no more fishing trips or cooking lessons. Ying had to tell the coach at the gymnastic studio that she would be unable to dance in the parade. She was so sad she hardly spoke.

And if Ying's sad attitude wasn't bad enough, Aunt Chan and Uncle Wu were on edge as they waited for the review from Mrs. Liu in the *Hong Kong Dining Authority*. It'd been three days since her visit, and Aunt Chan and Uncle Wu kept checking the website but nothing had appeared yet.

"I'm not sure what's worse," Aunt Chan wondered, "a

poor review or no review at all?"

"At least with a bad review, people will know we're here," Uncle Wu said. "Maybe they'll make up their own minds and give us a try, anyway."

"But no review means no one will read about the Golden Lion. They won't know we're here," Aunt Chan said.

"We have to do something," Emilia said as they folded napkins. She watched as Ying wiped a table. "Look at Ying—she's so quiet and miserable, I don't know what to say to her. She's acting like her life is over."

"What are we supposed to do?" Alfie asked. "The only thing that'll make her happy is gymnastics and being in the parade tomorrow, but we can't go against her parents. They grounded her."

"But don't you think this is too important?" Emilia asked. "Mrs. Liu has already been here. There's nothing anyone can do about it now. If we help Ying get into the parade—"

"They said no more gymnastics," Alfie reminded her.

"They said no more going to the *gym*," Emilia said with a sneaky smile. "That doesn't mean she can't do gymnastics or practice somewhere else for the parade."

"True . . . ," Alfie said.

"If we can help her slip out for one more rehearsal and then help her get to the parade without her parents knowing, just think how they'll feel when they see the junior lion dance coming down the street and find out it's their daughter. They'll be so happy."

"Or they'll ground her for life," Alfie said.

"Well, I'm willing to risk it," she said.

"Yeah," Alfie said. "I guess."

That evening, in the girls' bedroom, they told Ying their plan.

"All this hard work you've done," Emilia said as Ying thought it over. "You can't quit now."

"I'm not quitting," Ying said. "I never quit."

"Okay, so don't give up now. We want to help you."

"That's very nice. But don't bother. Mother and Father are too angry with me and too worried about the restaurant for me to rock the boat. I'm not sure they'll ever forgive me."

"You're their daughter," Emilia said. "Of course they'll forgive you. Once they see how dedicated you are to the dance, they'll understand how much discipline and determination you have. This could change everything!"

"Everything except the restaurant review," Ying said.

"This is the one thing we can control," Alfie said. "We'll totally cover for you. Just give it this one last chance. Your parents can't punish you any more than they already have, right?"

"Well . . . ," Ying began. "I guess that's a good point. Okay. Tell me your plan again."

The next day, Ying was there to help out all through the lunch service, which was brisk, and the restaurant was more than half full of customers. This helped put a small smile on Aunt Chan's face.

Once lunch was over, everyone set about cleaning up. As Aunt Chan went over the day's receipts and Uncle Wu busied himself with inventory for the next day, Ying slipped out the front door to prepare for the parade.

Luckily, Ying's parents were so busy with the details of the restaurant that when they called for Ying to do something they hardly looked up.

"Ying! Please check there are full bottles of soy sauce on every table!" Uncle Wu called from the pantry.

"She's on it," Alfie called as he went to check the tables.

"Ying! Where's Ying?" Aunt Chan called. "She needs to restock the bathroom."

"She's taking the trash out," Emilia said. "I'll tell her when she gets back." Emilia then restocked the bathroom.

The plan was for Ying to rehearse, then come back

before the family left together for the parade, then slip off just before she needed to line up and get into costume. As Aunt Chan and Uncle Wu finished up for the afternoon, Alfie and Emilia started to worry that Ying wouldn't be back in time and the whole plan would fall apart.

"Everybody ready?" Aunt Chan asked, pulling on her coat. "Wait. Where's Ying?"

Emilia looked around nervously, and Alfie was just about to spill the beans when his sister suddenly said, "She's right here."

Ying had snuck in from the back. Her cheeks were pink—she must have run all the way from the rehearsal.

"Oh," Aunt Chan said, giving her a double take. "I didn't see you there."

Ying smiled. "Just checking that everything was done."

The streets were filled with crowds of people still celebrating as they walked happily along the sidewalks, just as they had the evening Alfie and Emilia arrived. From far away, they could hear the beating drums of

dances in other parts of the city.

Ying prepared for her escape. She stayed in the back as the family worked to find the best spot to view the parade.

"Right here!" Ying said suddenly. To Alfie and Emilia she whispered, "This is where we finish. It'll be perfect if they can see me here."

Aunt Chan and Uncle Wu crowded in shoulder-to-shoulder with the others to await the start of the parade. Ying made sure she was at a distance from her parents in the hopes that they wouldn't notice whether she was standing with them.

The parade started and the crowd began to cheer. Since they were at the end of the line, they—and Ying— had to wait a few minutes for the parade to make its way down the streets to them. As soon as the first part of the parade had passed, Ying took off.

"See you at the end," she said.

Chapter 15

There was plenty to distract Aunt Chan and Uncle Wu—
as well as Alfie and Emilia. Large groups of dancers came
down the parade line in matching red, pink, and white
costumes with bright Chinese umbrellas; groups in
traditional costumes with their faces painted did more
dances and routines; parade floats were covered in lights
top to bottom, casting a festive glow across the entire
crowd.

"The lions are coming!" Emilia said, pointing and
jumping.

A throng of drummers led the procession, along with
several hand percussionists clapping cymbals the size of

dinner plates. Alfie felt the beating in his chest, rhythmic and exhilarating.

Alfie could just spot the white of the lion costume coming toward them. The head of the lion swayed back and forth, bounced down the street, and fluttered its eyelids, all to the beat of the drummers. Aunt Chan and Uncle Wu clapped their hands along to the music.

One lion stopped just in front of the family to perform. The costume was made of a delicate fabric that fluttered gracefully with every movement. Ying's legs acted as the front legs of the lion. Hidden underneath, she used her arms to move the head, work the eyes, and even work the ears. Her partner, Ju, was the back legs of the lion and had to be in perfect sync with the front to make it look like a larger-than-life lion brought to life.

Alfie and Emilia stood transfixed as Ying and Ju did their dance. Ying made the lion's head look directly at Aunt Chan and Uncle Wu and flutter its eyes before turning back into the street and continuing its dance.

When the performance ended, the crowd gave them enthusiastic applause.

"Wasn't that amazing?" Alfie asked Aunt Chan and Uncle Wu.

"Very impressive for such young dancers," Uncle Wu said.

"Lots of training," Alfie added. "And talent."

"And dedication," Emilia added.

"It's nice to see young people so committed to an ancient tradition," Aunt Chan said. "I wonder if Ying— Ying?"

At that moment, Ying removed the head of lion to take her bow along with Ju. Alfie clapped so hard his hands hurt, and he couldn't stop smiling. When he turned to look at Ying's parents, her mother wore an expression of disbelief while Uncle Wu's eyes looked a bit teary. It was the perfect reaction.

Ying stepped closer to her parents. She waved good-bye to Ju, who went to find her own family.

"Well, surprise," Ying said to her parents.

"Ying, I can't believe that was you," Aunt Chan said. "Is this what you've been doing all this time you weren't at the restaurant?"

"Yes," Ying said. "I'm sorry I deceived you. Honestly. I just felt like you didn't understand how important this is

to me. And how good I am at it. At least, I
think I am."

"You are," Uncle Wu
said. "You are incredibly
talented, Ying."

"It was
wonderful, Ying.
Although we're not
happy about your
sneaking off," Aunt Chan said. "And I certainly don't like
being deceived by my daughter. That said—you were
amazing. Ying, we're so proud of you."

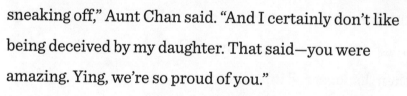

Ying, her mother, and her father all huddled in for a
tight hug. Emilia could hardly contain her happiness and
clapped as she hopped up and down.

"Pardon me," a familiar voice said. They all turned
to see Mrs. Liu standing in front of them. Alfie worried
that the family would be uncomfortable seeing the
woman that held the fate of their restaurant in her hands,

but Aunt Chan and Uncle Wu looked surprisingly calm. He supposed they were too busy being amazed by their daughter.

"Hello, Mrs. Liu," Uncle Wu said. "Did you enjoy the parade?"

"Very much," she said. "Especially this girl's lion dance. Very impressive."

Ying smiled proudly. "Thank you."

"Well," Mrs. Liu said, pausing to look at each member of the family, "have a good evening." Mrs. Liu looked at Ying and grasped her hand, whispered something to her, and then disappeared into the crowd.

"That was weird," Alfie said as they watched her walk away.

Ying ran back to find her instructor to return her costume. She was able to change quickly and come back to meet the family. "Let's get some food," she said. "I'm starving."

"Your mother and I will get treats," Uncle Wu said.

"Why don't you find a place to sit?"

"Father, wait," Ying said. She whispered something in his ear.

"You sure?" Uncle Wu asked her.

"Definitely," she said.

Ying, Alfie, and Emilia walked through the crowds and miraculously found an open bench overlooking the harbor, which was filled with boats covered in lights for the festival. They sat down and looked out at the water and skyscrapers of Kowloon.

"Looks like we did it," Ying said.

"Yep," Alfie said.

"Thank you both so much for helping me," Ying said. "It means so much to me."

"Of course," Emilia said. "You're so talented, how could we not?"

Ying smiled. "Well, next we eat sticky rice balls and hang out for a while. Watch the fireworks. Tomorrow everything goes back to normal."

Alfie looked at his sister. "I wonder."

Uncle Wu and Aunt Chan returned with a plastic bag full of sticky rice balls.

"This is another new year's tradition," Uncle Wu said as he opened the bag. "These are called *tang yuan*, and they can have all different kinds of fillings, like walnuts, fish, tangerine peel, black-bean paste, and even green beans or rose petals."

Uncle Wu passed around the plastic bag of rice balls, which looked like Ping-Pong balls.

"Sesame paste!" said Ying of the first one she grabbed. "My favorite!"

Alfie bit into one. It was soft but firm and the center held a sweet taste of almond.

Emilia took a bite of hers.

"I'm not sure what it is, but it's delicious!" she said.

"You got one with shredded pork," Aunt Chan said, looking at the rice ball in Emilia's hand.

Everyone's hands dove into the bag for seconds while Uncle Wu explained to Alfie and Emilia why it was important to eat them on this last day of the Spring Festival.

He held one up and said, "Looks like a full moon, doesn't it? It symbolizes family unity and wholeness, which is very important. And which is why, Ying, there's still something we must discuss with you."

"This is the part when the night goes bad, isn't it?" Ying said.

"I'm afraid you're not going to be happy," Uncle Wu said.

Alfie braced himself along with Ying and Emilia. They were ready to hear what Aunt Chan and Uncle Wu had to say.

Chapter 16

Uncle Wu began by saying, "Your mother and I discussed this, and we've come to some decisions."

Alfie watched Ying's face as she tried to stay positive.

"We do not appreciate—or tolerate—being deceived," Aunt Chan said. "However—we're sorry. We were so focused on the restaurant that we never really asked what you wanted. And you clearly want to keep up your training."

"More than anything," Ying said.

"So this is what we feel will be fair," Uncle Wu said. "You will take a week off from gymnastics and during that week you will help out at the restaurant just as we've expected you to. How does that sound?"

"Totally fair," Ying said. "Thank you for understanding. Now if only I could do something about the restaurant review."

"Well," Uncle Wu sighed, "we'll deal with that when it happens."

Ying smiled as she reached into her coat pocket and pulled out a folded piece of paper. "Mrs. Liu slipped this to me after the parade. It's the review—she said it goes up on the website tonight."

Aunt Chan took the piece of paper from Ying and carefully unfolded it. She took a deep breath and began reading: "'The charming family-owned restaurant, which is surrounded by flashy, more expensive venues, specializes in what the people of Hong Kong do best— fish. It is a no-frills approach that highlights the quality of the fish and delicate handling of its preparation.'"

"It's a good review!" said Uncle Wu.

"'The family seems to know what you want even if you

think you know otherwise,'" Aunt Chan continued. "'As any good restaurateur knows, fresher is always better, and the Golden Lion delivered the freshest scallops I have ever tasted.'" Aunt Chan was on the verge of tears.

"We've done it," Uncle Wu said to her. "Now all we can do is keep working as hard as we have been, and success will come to us."

Aunt Chan smiled. "Yes, you're right," she said, folding the review back and tucking it into her pocket. Uncle Wu put his arm around her and gave a gentle squeeze. Aunt Chan turned to smile at him and the strain and stress of the past few days seemed to melt away.

"Oh, Ying," Uncle Wu said. "I picked up that special

item you asked for." He handed her a bag.

"Perfect!" Ying said. "Alfie, this is for you." From the bag she pulled out what appeared to be a hard-boiled egg, the color a bit brown instead of gleaming white.

"What is it?" Alfie asked, because he knew it wasn't just an egg. Ying was up to something.

"You said you'd try anything," she said. "How about a thousand-year-old egg?"

"It's not really that old, is it?" Emilia asked.

"No," Ying said. "More like a hundred days. That's a duck egg. They preserve it in a clay mixture with ash, salt, and lime. You up for it?" Ying held the egg out to Alfie.

He took the egg from Ying. The shell was still on it, so he cracked it on the edge of the bench. If he thought the outside of the egg was strangely colored, he wasn't prepared for what he saw inside. "It's totally black!"

"I'm going to be sick," Emilia said.

"Keep going," Ying said, with a devilish smile.

As he continued to peel off the shell, the smell began

to escape—a rotten smell, like sulfur. The egg itself was like a gummy candy. If gummy candy was black and stinky.

"It's like Jell-O," Alfie said. "What are you trying to do to me? It smells awful."

Emilia held her nose while Ying laughed.

Alfie pulled the egg apart. The smell was like rotten meat. The yolk was green and black slime.

"It looks like zombie brains," Emilia said through her pinched nose.

"I'm going for it," Alfie said bravely.

Alfie took a bite. His stomach immediately lurched but he kept going. The yolk was creamy and a little salty but other than that he didn't taste much. It was the smell that kept overwhelming his senses. He managed to get one bite down then threw up his hands.

"I can't do the rest," he said. His eyes were watering. "Get that thing away from me," he coughed.

Ying laughed and took the rest of the egg to the nearest trash can. Emilia kept her nose pinched until it was far away.

"I don't know if you're brave," Emilia said, "or stupid."

"Stupid, definitely," Alfie said, coughing again. "But at least I did it."

"Well done!" Ying said when she came back and sat down. "Now you've eaten something that even some locals won't touch."

"Great," Alfie said, but he didn't feel great. "Are there any more of those sticky rice balls? That might help get the taste of the egg out of my mouth."

Ying got the bag and handed it around. "I've been a terrible friend," she said.

"Yeah, what kind of friend forces you to eat that kind of stuff?" Alfie said, smiling.

"Not that," Ying said. "I mean, I've never even asked you about your family. I've been so selfish while you were here. What are they like?"

Emilia reached into the bag for another treat and said, "I guess they're like yours. Strict but fair."

"*Sometimes* they're fair," Alfie said.

"Yeah, they're totally unfair when Alfie is trying to get away with something," Emilia said.

"Like me?" Ying joked. "Do you miss them?"

"We've been so busy here I hadn't thought much about it," Alfie said. The truth was, he and Emilia missed their parents and Zia Donatella whenever they were off on an adventure, but they knew they'd go back at some point—they just never knew when. "Hong Kong has been amazing, but it will be good to be home again."

"Ying! Come look!" Aunt Chan said. She and Uncle Wu leaned over the railing and were looking out at the boats together. Ying ran to her parents.

Alfie and Emilia sat quietly thinking. Alfie was sure his sister was thinking the same thing he was—that no matter how many times they went away, or how much fun they had, or how much they learned, they were always happy to get back home to their family.

"You know what these remind me of?" Emilia said as she took another sticky rice ball out of the bag that sat between them. Alfie reached in for another as well. "They're like the *arancini* Mom and Zia Donatella make—those yummy little fried rice balls filled with mozzarella."

"Yeah, you're right," Alfie said. He took a bite of the sticky rice ball. "It's strange how food from such totally different cultures could be so similar. When Zia made the *arancini*, I thought it was the greatest invention of all time."

"I know," Emilia said. "I think Dad ate about a dozen."

"He's been so interested in food since Zia's come to live with us. Maybe we should ask him to help us cook something for Mom when we get back," Alfie said.

As they sat silently, feeling the breeze on their cheeks and hearing the laughter of families celebrating the new year, Alfie got that feeling in his stomach, the same one that got him here. He reached out for his sister's hand, clasping it tightly.

Chapter 17

Alfie opened his eyes and saw his sister looking around their kitchen with a startled look on her face. They were back in their kitchen, the plate of scallion pancakes still on the counter. Just like before, although they had been gone for days, but no time had passed at home.

"We never get to say good-bye," Emilia said.

"Maybe next time we can figure out a way to do it differently. Come on," he said as he looked at the clock on the wall. "It's the middle of the night. Let's go to bed."

The next morning started off the way a perfect Saturday should—sleeping in late and waking up to the smell of bacon frying.

"Good morning, sleepyhead," Mom said as Alfie dragged himself into the kitchen. Emilia was at the counter arranging bacon on a paper-towel-covered plate. Dad leaned against the counter drinking coffee while Mom fried the bacon and Zia mixed batter.

"Sleep well?" Zia asked, turning to smile at him.

"I feel like I've been asleep for a week," Alfie said.

"Load me up on whatever you're making there, Zia Donatella," Dad said. "I've got an entire garage to clean out while these two kids mess around all day."

"I told you I have a school project," Emilia said.

"And Alfie wants to play soccer, I know," Dad said. He smiled and said, "I'm only teasing you both. The garage is my project, not yours."

Alfie and Emilia looked at each other. Sure, the project was their dad's, but they could help out. It might even be fun to do it together—go through all the old boxes and see what they wanted to save and what they wanted to toss.

"Maybe we can help you," Alfie said.

"Yeah, we'll help," Emilia said. "If Mom helps, too."

"I'd be happy to join you," Mom replied. "That garage needs a serious cleaning."

"And I'll help by making you this wonderful breakfast," Zia said.

"What are you making?" Alfie asked.

"Crepes," Zia said.

Emilia sat up and said, "Like the ones in Paris?"

"Yes, like Paris," Zia replied. "And other places. Paris isn't the only place where you can get them. There are lots of places that have been influenced by the French."

"What about in America?" Alfie asked.

"Sure," Zia said. She poured a small amount of the thin batter into a hot skillet. "Places like New Orleans, in Louisiana."

"I've read about that," Emilia said. When Alfie looked at her doubtfully she said, "No, really. I've read about the French Quarter."

"So are you making those crepes New Orleans style?" Alfie asked.

"Yes, I am," Zia said. "They're filled with eggs, goat cheese, and crawfish. Interested in trying?"

Alfie wasn't sure about the combination, but he was always interested in trying Zia's food. Plus he'd never been to New Orleans.

"Definitely interested," Alfie said.

A Note from Giada

My younger sister and I have traveled together to places all over the world, but Hong Kong took our breath away like nowhere else. Nicknamed "the Pearl of the Orient," the city is like no other. It started out as a small fishing village, became a stop on several trading routes, and is now a spectacular international city known for finance and food. Nestled amid lush rolling hills, the city is like a box of crayons with its buildings in every color imaginable. And at night the whole city comes alive with a dazzling light show.

During our trip we were never hungry and ate everything from dumplings to curries to the tastiest little cakes I've ever had. My favorite was a rice dumpling with spiced chicken in the center wrapped in a banana leaf. It was like a little present of deliciousness and I couldn't wait to get home and re-create the dish for my family.

No trip to Hong Kong is complete without a bit of shopping. The city has every kind of market, and my favorite was, of course, the jade market. I bought myself a jade necklace on a red string, and every time I wear it I can close my eyes and be transported right back to that magical city. My daughter, Jade, asks to wear my necklace, and when she's old enough I'll certainly want to share it with her, as well as the fabulous city it came from.

Xo